W4   99p

D1374862

Gran's Gang Solve a Mystery

To Raman

Best wishes

Susan Townsend

ADRIAN TOWNSEND

Gran's Gang Solve a Mystery

Illustrated by Kate Chesterton

First Published 2008 By
Grassy Hill Publishing
52 Wheatley Road Garsington Oxford OX44 9ER

Text Copyright © 2008 Adrian Townsend
Illustrations Copyright © 2008 Kate Chesterton

All rights reserved; no part of this publication may be reproduced or transmitted by any means, electronic, mechanical, photographic, or otherwise, without the prior permission of the publisher.

The moral right of the author has been asserted.

ISBN 978-1-903569-08-5

Contents

Gran's Gang
Solve a Mystery

My gran is a famous detective. At least she thinks she is. She and the rest of her gang Ada, Ethel, Winnie and Nora, have all been in the local paper. They had their pictures taken as well. *"Grandmothers solve local mystery,"* said the headline. My mum said gran "got lucky" but I think she knew what she was doing. My gran can do anything, my gran's a hero.

It all started when she and everyone else got back from their group holiday in Spain. Mum took Gran away for some 'bonding' and they ended up

taking most of the street with them.
Mum was worried before she went
because not everyone gets on with my
gran and her gang, especially Basil
Wainwright, Ethel's next door
neighbour. But everyone got on fine.
Donna from next door said they were
all "full of it" when they got back.
"The best holiday ever," said Winnie.
She'd had to miss two weeks of her
basketball training just to go but she
said "the break had done her good"
and she's now joint top basket scorer
in her league.
Nora said it was "sunshine heaven."
She said she learnt some new 'Spanish
techniques' for her roller blading. She

says she can now do one foot gliders all the way to the bus stop. My mum says Nora has become a menace. The pavements are no longer safe when she's in one of her roller blading moods.

Gran brought some new gear back with her including some leather trousers and she's been fiddling with her mixing deck for ages. She says that Spanish music mixed into hip-hop will be the next big thing in the clubs. I'm not sure what she's talking about, especially "retro-garage" and "80's base line" but it seems to keep her happy so I just smile, nod and say "yes, Gran." So my mum and everyone else had a great time on holiday. But, the best bit is that Ethel became friends with Basil and Betty Wainwright. They had spent 20 years arguing and bickering over their garden fence and they all came back from Spain the best of mates. Ethel said the holiday was "the trip of a lifetime" and she didn't just mean the race down the mountain in a Spanish go-cart. She said that if she could drive really fast with Basil Wainwright sitting next to her she'd never worry about losing speed when she goes banger racing again. She's even given Basil a nickname "Basil the Banger" she calls him and here's the best bit; Basil doesn't mind. He just

smiles and says "OK Petrol Ethel."
Betty Wainwright's not too sure about
this but she does agree that the holiday
was great. She says it was important
that the Vicar was with them for
spiritual guidance. My mum says that
Betty Wainwright discovered the
spiritual effects of Spanish fruit juice.
Spain is a powerful place.
Anyway, the holiday went well for
everyone. They all came back happy
and refreshed. You can sense the
difference down our street Nora shouts
"Olé" as she passes you on her roller
blades. Winnie bounces up and down
her driveway with her basketball, "un,
dos, tres, Basket!" can be heard all

down our street and Gran's garage "music" leaks out of her garage. As for Ethel, Basil and Betty, they've started having coffee mornings together and Spanish barbecue evenings. Things were going so well until something mysterious happened.

The Mystery Begins

It was Friday evening, and Basil and Betty were getting ready for another Spanish barbecue. A few weeks had gone by since they'd got back from Spain and they'd got into the habit of cooking outdoors "just like the Spanish." Betty had found that she could buy Spanish "fruit juice" in a local supermarket. It was only two extra stops on the bus and she thought it was worth it to get the juice because she, Basil and Ethel all agreed that the Spanish evenings went better with a few glasses of it to remind them of Spain. This particular Friday, Basil thought it would be a good idea to invite a few friends who'd been on the trip to Spain with them. "After all tomorrow is mañana," said Basil as he suggested the idea to Betty. "I've got some really good peppers that have come on in the garden and the tomatoes are brilliant this year. If the sun shines it will be just like we're in Spain," he said to Ethel as they talked about the idea. So phone calls were made and a number of people who had been on the trip to Spain said they could attend. Only Wally Coulter, the Rodgers and Bob Yates couldn't make it and the Vicar had to cancel at the last minute as an urgent Parish matter came up unexpectedly. Mary Whitefleet was disappointed. Gran, Nora and Winnie all said they could go and mum said she ought to go "just to keep an eye on things."

Basil, Betty and Ethel spent all afternoon getting ready. Basil picked his peppers and tomatoes. He cut the grass and re-arranged his garden gnome collection so that they too looked like they were in the party mood. He paid particular attention to Fisherman Freddy, a cheery looking, fat gnome with a beard. He's got a red shiny pointy head and a blue jacket painted on him. He sits on a stool and holds a long fishing rod over a blue

and yellow concrete well. Next to the
well is a small sign that Basil made out
of concrete. He also made letters for
the sign by sticking different coloured
pebbles to make letters and words. The
sign next to the well says, "Fisherman
Freddy's Fishing well." When Basil is

really pleased with something in his garden he likes to make a little pebble sign for it. He's got other signs next to some of his other gnomes; there's "Wilber with his wheelbarrow," "Peter with his pipe", "Lillie and her lamp," "Resting on toadstools," "Susie on her swing" and Basil's favourite gnome "Phil the Irish fluter". Basil has even made a pebble sign that stands just outside his front door, "There's no place like gnome," says the sign as you walk up the front path. Lots of people who walk past Basil and Betty's house peer over the fence to admire Basil's garden. Most of them smile and chuckle as they read the signs and view his garden ornaments. My mum shakes her head and raises her eyebrows.

Basil decided that "Fisherman Freddy" should be placed at the front of the lawn close to the pathway to welcome people as they arrive at the Spanish barbecue. He gave Freddy an extra polish and moved him close to the gate. Then he got some extra coloured pebbles from his back garden and laid them out on the lawn to welcome people. The greeting said:

"Fisherman Freddy is fishing well. Welcome to the barbecue, life is really swell."

Basil was so pleased with his

handiwork that he gave all the other gnomes an extra polish. He even re-painted "Phil the Irish Fluter's" flute so that it looked like real gold. When he'd finished, Basil thought he deserved a rest, so he put his big sack of coloured pebbles behind his apple tree and had a snooze in his deck chair.

Betty was at work in the kitchen. She was preparing the peppers and tomatoes ready to be eaten later. She was just washing her third bowl of lovely ripe tomatoes when she heard a voice. "Shake a leg," shouted Ada, "Shake a leg and get ready to rock. I've got the entertainment for this evening."

Ada was pulling a large trolley on wheels with a massive box on it. "I've brought my mixing decks," Ada said to Betty. "I've got some great new mixes, hip-hop with Spanish cool. This will get them dancing tonight."

"Oh Ada, I'm not sure we…" Betty began, but Ada didn't stop to listen. "I'll just put this lot down here while I take the trolley back for my amplifier" said Ada. Betty still wasn't sure.

"Amplifier? Do we need that? What about the neighbours?" asked Betty, but Ada was half way back up the garden path. "Neighbours, everybody needs good neighbours" she sang. While Betty returned to her tomatoes,

Ethel was busy getting ready next door. "Now where is that blooming thing?" said Ethel to herself. "I know it's here somewhere. If lost things had tongues, they'd be able to talk and tell you where they are. That's what my Auntie Nellie used to say to me. Come on now speak to me. Where are you?"

Ethel was in her garage looking for a piece of equipment she called a Christmas tree. It isn't a real tree, it's a big metal stack of lights, red, yellow and green. Ethel had got it from a local drag racing circuit after the drag racing company went bankrupt. She'd only paid £40 for it. It was used to tell the drag cars when it was time to start a race; red for stop, yellow to get ready and green for GO.

"Come on now, where are you? Let's be having you. Don't be shy." Ethel moved old bits of car engines, hub caps, old tyres and cans of paint. Finally she pulled at a large oily sheet and there it was.

"Bingo!" said Ethel, "This will light up the party," and she dragged the lights out of the garage. "It's even got its stand. This was a bargain." Ethel said to herself. "Now where's me generator." Ethel went back into her garage to rummage some more. Just as she did Nora came racing into her driveway on her rollerblades.

"Look lively," she shouted. "Ethel, are you in there? Is old Basil from next door still doing the barbecue thing this evening? I've just had a brilliant idea." Ethel came out of the garage dragging her Christmas tree.

"What's that?" said Nora, stopping sharply.

"It's me *drag racing* Christmas tree," said Ethel.

"Does it work?" asked Nora.

"It will if I can find the blooming generator."

"Wow, I bet it gives off plenty of light. Can you make it flash?" asked Nora.

"Sure can," said Ethel. "If I can find the generator."

"Well if you can get it going that would be great because I've had an idea too. You see I thought we could have a roller blade disco dancing competition tonight at the barbecue. It might liven things up a bit. Ada says she can sort the music. Harry Thistlewaite says he can get some flat boarding. We can put it on Basil's lawn and use his path as well, that's nice and smooth. I've even got some spare roller blades for people to borrow. All we need are the lights."

"Well you might have to whistle for them. I can't find the blooming generator," shouted Ethel, from back in the garage. "It's useless without it."

"Why don't you just plug it into the

mains electricity?" asked Nora.

"Because drag racing takes place in the middle of a field Nora," said Ethel. "There is no electricity in the middle of fields. They run the lights off generators. Sometimes they connect things up to their car engines with belts and things but without something to power it this light set is useless. Ethel and Nora both stared at the useless Christmas tree.

"You two need to get some exercise you know," came a voice from the end of the drive. It was Winnie out on her daily fitness jog. "You don't get to be top of the league by standing about you know." Winnie jogged up the driveway and kept running in circles around Nora and Ethel as she spoke to them. "Well, what are you doing?" asked Winnie.

"Trying to see how we can get this light tree to work," said Nora.

"We can't get power to it," said Ethel. "I can't find the generator."

Winnie jogged around the light tree again. "Well I don't know anything about cars Ethel but I think this thing's got a plug on it. Look here! I think that's where you can plug it into the mains." Ethel prodded her finger where Winnie was pointing.

"You're absolutely right, Winnie. Brilliant! I've never noticed that before.

This could be just the ticket. Hang on, I'll get a lead and plug it in," said Ethel.

Ada returned with her amplifier just as Winnie turned on the lights.

"Wow!" said Nora as a host of red, yellow and green lights lit up the driveway.

"Brilliant," said Winnie as she carried on jogging.

"That's the ticket," said Ethel. "But the lights are supposed to flash on and off."

"Oh don't worry about that," said Ada. "I can connect it up to my base-pulse unit. I can make the lights flash on and off in time to my music."

"I think we're in for a good time at the Spanish barbecue tonight ladies," said Winnie.

"Wicked," said the gang.

At six o'clock most people had arrived at the barbecue. Basil was very proud of the way he had set out his garden gnomes and he thought his pebble signs were a great idea.

"I think the garden looks lovely dearest" said Betty. "You've invited all our little gnome friends as well," and she kissed Basil on the cheek.

Basil blushed with embarrassment but he was pleased with himself. Not only had he arranged the gnomes but he had also cleared a space for Nora's rollerblading dance floor. He'd found some real Christmas tree lights and decorations and hung them up in his apple tree. Mary Whitefleet gave Basil some candle lanterns from the church and Mum found a large Spanish flag. She hung it out of Basil and Betty's bedroom window. The barbecue looked very festive.

"It will look even better when it gets dark," said Ethel. "We'll have quite a light show later."

Ada was busy at her mixing desk. She was keeping the music in the background.

"We'll let everybody eat and drink first," said Ada. "I'll keep it cool at first and tweak it up later."

The party was moving along. Basil was so proud of his party that he waved to strangers as they walked past his house. Most of them just waved back, some of them even shouted "Olé" and did a little dance. It was only Morgan Stansfield who didn't seem pleased. Morgan lives in the next street to Winnie and his house backs onto Basil and Betty's house. He stopped at the gate and exchanged some angry words with Basil. Mum tried to listen but against the music all she heard was "should know better" and "people of your age." After a while, Morgan walked off.

"Right then everybody," announced
Ada over her microphone. "Time to
move up a gear. It's time for some hip-
hop Spanish roller blade mixes. My
friends Nora and Winnie will
demonstrate on our new dance floor
how to do this. Then I want you all to

join in." Ada turned up the music and Nora roller bladed around the dance floor while Winnie bounced up and down. "Join in everyone," they shouted, "join in."

Gran knew it was time to hit the switch on Ethel's drag racing lights. As the lights came on everyone cheered and Mum said the whole street was lit up. Everyone began to dance, some on the dance floor, others danced up and down Basil's pathway

"Let's make them flash," said Ada and she turned on her base pulse unit. The lights flashed red, yellow and green, and everyone cheered. Then silence and darkness; only the glow of the candle lanterns lit up the shadows in the garden. There was not a single light in the entire street. All the house lights were out as well as the street lamps. Every house was in darkness.

"Must have been a power cut," said Ada.

"Or it was my lights," said Ethel. "I wasn't too sure about connecting them to the mains."

"Oh no!" said Ada, "We were just starting to swing. Can you do anything about it?"

"Give me your torch," said Ethel. "I'll just pop in the garage and see what I can do."

The light from two more torches

glowed as they stopped at Basil's gateway. Morgan Stansfield had returned with his wife, Julia, and they'd brought Councillor Bolam with them. Everyone knew he was the Chairman of the Parish Council. It was very quiet now so most people heard bits of what Councillor Bolam said to Basil. He mentioned complaints about elderly hooligans and items for the agenda for the next Parish meeting. Mary Whitefleet was hiding behind the apple tree. She definitely heard "anti-social neighbours" and "asbo". Eventually Julia Stansfield said something about "property values" and all three walked off together. Mum started to stack up glasses and half-eaten plates of food. Donna suggested to Ada that it was probably time to pack up.

"I've never liked those Stansfields," said Ada. "He's an accountant and she's an estate agent."

"What's that got to do…" Donna started to reply, but she was stopped by the sound of a revving car engine next door. Ethel had started her hot rod car. She revved the engine louder four more times. This was followed by the bright lights of the drag racing Christmas tree and the sound of Ada's music.

Ethel had rigged up her car to generate

the lights and music. Everyone cheered. Ada got into action.

"OK everyone" she announced. "We're back in business. Time for the Spanish one two three, uno, dos, tres," she called. Everyone danced in time to the music as the lights changed red, yellow and green. Uno, dos, tres.

Ada was in her stride, she started to use her mixing decks. She faded in some Spanish garage music, then a snatch of a tango. Everyone was back on their feet singing and bouncing around Basil's garden.

"This is the thing," said Ada and she started to think about what new sounds she could mix into the music.

Suddenly she heard a new sound, but it was not one of her own. It was the siren of an approaching police car. The flashing blue lights added a new effect to the light tree; blue-red, blue-yellow, blue-green. Two policemen jumped out of their car. One went straight up to Basil Wainwright and the other ran to Ada.

"I think we'll stop that now love," he said.

Mum said she'd never been so humiliated. "In all my time, I've never been in trouble with the police," she said. "Poor Betty, she was mortified. She didn't know where to look when that policeman said he'd arrest her if she didn't start clearing away and tell her guests to go home," said Mum. Mum told the policeman that she'd stay and help tidy things up. She and Mary Whitefleet got most of the plates and glasses indoors, while Gran, Nora, Ethel and Winnie quickly loaded Gran's disco gear onto her trolley. They pushed it into Ethel's garage, quickly followed by Ethel's light tree. Ethel locked her garage door, and by the time the policeman had wandered around the garden telling people to go home, Gran and her gang were picking up bits of litter and pretending to help tidy up.

"Where did that disco unit go?" asked

a policeman.

"I don't know," said Gran. "I think some young lad popped it into a white van. They pulled off a couple of minutes ago. You just missed them."

"Are you sure?" asked the other policeman. "I think I recognise you. Don't you do a regular set down at the Silver Stars night club?"

"Don't be silly! At my age!" said Gran. "Though it's nice of you to think I'm still groovy officer." Betty nudged Ada with her elbow.

"No, no you're wrong young man" said Gran. "This is the first time I've had a night out in ages."

The policeman said nothing but looked

long and hard at Ada.

"Well," he eventually said. "Your night out is over. You'd best get yourself home. You too ladies," he said to Ethel, Winnie and Nora.

"Very well," said Winnie. "Thank you for your help. We're all glad the noise has stopped, aren't we girls? I don't know what this neighbourhood is coming to." And with that, Ada and the gang hot-footed it away from the scene.

Ada and Ethel were particularly pleased to have hidden their equipment from the police. They both knew it could have been confiscated, so to be on the safe side, Ada left it quite late the next morning to go around to Ethel's house to get her mixing deck. That was when she walked into more trouble.

Winnie was also on her way to Ethel's house. She had just finished her morning basketball practice. She dribbled up to Gran and bounced the ball around her before running up to the next lamp post and bouncing the ball off it.

"Are you going to do that all the way to Ethel's?" asked Ada.

"Practice. Practice Ada, it's the only thing that keeps me on top. Anyway what are you so grumpy about? You got away with it last night, you could have lost your stuff to the police you know."

"I know," said Ada.

"It's a good job we got it out of sight quickly. I suppose I won't be happy until I've got it home safe and sound."

"Safe and sound, safe and sound, take the ball round, take the ball round," sang Winnie as she dribbled around another lamp post.

Together they walked and dribbled into Ethel's driveway.

"You've got a nerve!" shouted a voice from nowhere. It was Basil Wainwright from the other side of the fence.

"I thought you'd be hiding yourself away after the trouble you caused last night Ada. I've never been so humiliated in front of my neighbours and all because of your blooming racket."

"I don't do racket. Just cool music," Ada replied. "It's not my fault if you're too old to appreciate the latest scene Basil."

"Too old, too old am I? I thought you'd say that. I suppose you think it's funny that the police nearly arrested me instead of you?"

"Well, it was your party Basil"

"Party! It turned into a nightmare thanks to you and your bunch of... of... hooligans! It's bad enough living next door to Granny Drag Racer, but when you're all together it's like a mad house circus has come to town. Come on Betty, we don't want anything to do with them" and Basil took Betty down his garden into their greenhouse.

"What's got into him?" asked Winnie.

"I don't know," said Ethel, "but it started when he got up this morning. I heard him in his garden as usual and then I noticed him go around the front. "Whatever next," he shouted and Betty came dashing out of the house. Then all I could see was the pair of them dashing around their garden with a wheelbarrow. They were muttering and shouting and picking up stones. Betty saw me at the window and she shook her fist at me."

"Well something's got them rattled," said Ada. "I thought we were all getting along now."

"Not anymore," said Ethel, "and I don't know why."

"Oh I do," shouted Nora, as she roller bladed in from the street.

Nora had just got back from her early morning cleaning job. "I know what's up. Give me a coffee and I'll tell you all about it."

So, Gran and her gang all decamped for coffee inside Ethel's house, whilst Nora told them what she'd seen.

When Nora was getting up early as usual to go to work, she opened her curtains and in the half light she

thought she saw shapes moving around Basil's garden. She wasn't sure if it was a person or just shadows from the bushes and trees blowing in the breeze. Nora looked quite hard, but suddenly things stopped moving. She thought everything was alright, so she carried on getting ready for work. Later, when she'd put on her roller blades and was locking her back door she, thought she heard someone coughing in Basil's garden. "It's a bit early for Basil," she thought to herself.

Anyway, Nora roller bladed out of her drive and was sure she saw two shapes running round the corner further down the road. "They seemed in a bit of a hurry, but I didn't think anymore about it because I knew I could catch them up once I got my roller blades moving. The trouble was I didn't get going very quickly. I started off OK but when I got outside Basil's house I had to stop. That's when I saw it in his front garden."

"Saw what?" asked Ethel.

"The writing on his lawn; that precious lawn of his and all those blooming gnomes had been fiddled with. You know how he and Betty like to put those pebbles around the place so that they spell out notices and things. Well, someone must have got in and re-arranged them all. Right at the front of the lawn someone had written a notice in pebbles, it said: *'Wainwright's Badhouse. Stay away. No-one at Gnome.'*

Ethel, Winnie and Gran burst out laughing.

"No wonder he's like a bear with a sore head," said Gran. "Betty's

Badhouse, it's like a rap song," and
they all started to laugh again.

"I'm glad you think it's funny," said
Nora, "because the next bit is hilarious.
As well as the sign on the front lawn
there was another one on the other
side of the path, near the front door.
Whoever had done this had put four of
Basil's gnomes in a little group. One
gnome had an orange stuck onto the
point of its hat:

*'Winnie gnome, basketball basket
case'* said the sign.

Next to that was that silly gnome
sitting on a toadstool. The sign said:

*'Ethel gnome toadstool, grinning like
an old fool.'*

"Good grief," said Ethel.

"Then there was you Ada. You were that gnome on the swing," said Nora. "They had painted a bikini on the gnome, your sign said:

'Ada gnome, the oldest swinger in town'

"Old!" said Gran. "I'm not old; the very idea of it!"

Ethel, Winnie and Gran fell silent. They looked angry and sad. Eventually Ethel spoke.

"Hang on," she said." You said there were four gnomes in the group. What about the other one? That must have been you. What did they do for you?"

"Well," said Nora "I could hardly

believe it. You know I like my cleaning job and I like to get up early. I don't like laying around in bed. I always…"

"Yes, yes," said Gran. "Get on with it. What did they do to you?"

"They said I was like that silly gnome holding a lamp, and they'd made it look like I was trying to kiss another gnome, the one that looks like a troll. The sign said:

'Nora gnome, granny with the lamp. Always gets up early. Looking for a gramp.'

"I ask you, what a cheek! I've never been so insulted. If I'd had more time I'd have gone into the garden and kicked the stones around but I was late

for work so I had to get going. It's a
good job Basil has taken them away
otherwise he was going to get a piece
of my mind."

"Well, now we know" said Gran.

All of the gang were now quite angry.
They didn't like being insulted and
they didn't like the way Basil and Betty
had blamed them for what had
happened.

When Gran told my mum about it
Mum went to see the Wainwrights. She
found out that as well as all the
gnomes being moved about and the
pebble stones in the garden, Basil and
Betty discovered that two of their
gnomes were missing: 'Fisherman

Freddy' and Basil's favourite 'Phil the Irish fluter.'

"No wonder they're upset" said Mum. "They've had things stolen. Basil is convinced they took 'Phil the Fluter' because the thieves thought his flute was real gold."

Well, Mum talked with Basil and Betty for a long time. She persuaded them to go to the police. But apparently the police weren't very interested. Two of the officers remembered calling at the Wainwright's house about the noise.

"They didn't seem to care less," said Betty. "Anyone would think we were the criminals." But they did fill out a crime report form. At least Mum persuaded Basil and Betty that Gran and the gang had nothing to do with it all. Mum said the gang wouldn't have made silly signs about themselves if they had done it. Betty agreed, she said something about "being vain not stupid."

Mum's final idea was brilliant. She suggested that Basil and Betty should get together with the gang to see if they could find out who'd stolen the gnomes.

The Mystery Deepens.

Two days later the Wainwrights, the gang and one or two other people came to our house to work out a plan about how to get Basil's gnomes back. Mum was a sort of chairperson. The atmosphere was a bit frosty to start with, but Mum told everyone to "focus" and "stay positive". The vicar had come along and he said a few words about being a good neighbour and forgiving sinners, so eventually a 'plan of action' was drawn up.

It was agreed that Basil and Betty should design a lost and missing poster for the church notice board. Basil takes photos of all his gnomes, so he could put pictures of the missing gnomes on the poster with details about who to contact if anyone saw them. Everyone agreed this was a good idea and the vicar said he would draw attention to the poster in his daily services.

Ethel suggested that she should go around and fingerprint everyone in the street. She said it was a pity she didn't have a DNA kit and she wondered if she could borrow a lie detector to interrogate people with. She got quite excited until Winnie told her she watched too many crime dramas on TV and that most of what she was proposing was probably illegal.

"Immoral too," said the vicar, and he then said something about "casting the first stone," which Mum and Gran said was very funny because stones had actually caused the trouble in the first place.

Everybody laughed, except the vicar and Basil, even Mary Whitefleet smiled.

So the idea of a poster was adopted as the main and only plan of action. Basil produced the pictures and Mary Whitefleet did the typing. She printed it in colour and put it on the church notice board. The vicar mentioned it in his sermons for a week.

Nothing happened until a mysterious letter arrived at Basil and Betty's house some days later. It was addressed to *'The noisy gnome house'*. Inside was a message made up of cut out letters from a magazine, it said:

*"So you want your gnomes back.
Well, that gang of grannies you hang
out with will have to pay first. Wait
for further instructions."*

Basil and Betty didn't know what to
do. They wanted to go to the police,
but because they were so worried they
ended up telling Ethel all about it over
the garden fence. She told them to
hang on and she called Mum and the
gang to another meeting.

"This is getting serious," said Gran.

"We need to put a stop to this," said
mum, and they all looked at the note

trying to think who could have sent it.

"I've never liked that Mabel Pritchard," said Winnie. "She's jealous of my athletic powers. She told me once that basketball is not lady-like. I bet it's her. I've seen her tut tutting at me when I'm practising in the drive."

"Not for two months you haven't," said Nora. "She's in Malta with her youngest. She won't be back until November. It couldn't be her."

Well, what about Albert Higgins?" said Gran.

"Or Shirley Peachroft," said Winnie.

"And there's Margaret Bakewell. She's always…"

"Hold on, hold on," interrupted Mum.

"If you are going to make a list of all the people who don't like you or who are fed up of the way you behave, it's going to be a very long list!"

Gran and the gang looked at each other but said nothing.

"Look" said Mum. "I think we should keep a close eye on who is going in and out of Basil and Betty's house. If we could catch someone delivering the next note we'd have them red-handed. And we could do some careful observation of the area. This note looks like it's been made from the letters in one of those magazines that arrive with newspapers. Nora, you're up early, why don't you slow down a bit on your way to work and keep an eye on the newspapers that are delivered to people's houses. You could make a list. Ethel, you spend a lot of time in your garage. Why not work at the front with the door open where you can keep a close eye on anyone going into Basil and Betty's."

"Shall I make a list as well?" asked Ethel.

"You might as well," said Betty. "You seem to know everything we do anyway."

"Winnie," continued Mum, "You can get your friends in the basketball team to help. Get them to collect as many magazines as they can so that we can compare the letters and paper with the note."

"And what about me?" asked Gran.

"What am I going to do?"

"You're good with sounds," said Mum. "You can rig up a hidden microphone next to Basil and Betty's gate. We can listen in to what people are saying as they get close to Basil and Betty's house."

"I could probably record it on disc as well," said Gran.

"Even better," said Mum. "We'll meet again in three days' time to see what we've got."

"I think she's enjoying this," said Basil.

So the gang got to work.

Three days later they gathered in the Wainwright's house to compare notes. Winnie had a stack of magazines, Nora had a list, so did Ethel and Gran had a CD of dogs barking and traffic noise. "I'll have to do something about the ambient noises," she muttered.

"Right," said Mum. "What have we got?"

"Another note" said Betty as she came in with a tray of tea. "This note was in the hallway when I came back from the kitchen."

Everyone leapt to the window but there was no-one outside. Basil ran out of the front door. He came back puffing.

"No-one," he said. "How could I have

missed them?"

"I think I might have missed the note earlier," said Betty. "I only just noticed it under your shoes in the hallway, Basil."

"Well open it, what does it say?"asked Gran.

Basil began to read the note:

"Those grizzly grans have five forfeits. When they are done you get your gnomes back."

'Forfeit one: Ada.'
Tomorrow night at the Silver Stars' Ada must play a musical request: *'Please release me' by Engelbert Humperdinck,*

exactly at midnight."

"I can't do that," shrieked Gran. "Midnight on Friday, that's when the club is really steaming. *Engelbert Humperdinck.* I'll be a laughing stock. That music's for old people, I'll lose my gig slot."

"Hang on, hang on," said Mum. "What's number two?"

"Forfeit two: Winnie," said Basil "At Saturday's basketball match Winnie must miss two penalty shots in succession."

"Oh no!" said Winnie. "That's like match fixing. I'd rather give up basketball than cheat. You don't cheat in sport."

"You might not have to," said Ethel. "Aren't you playing Langrove Ladies? They're bottom of the league. You'll beat them easy, even if you miss two shots."

"But I haven't missed two penalties in succession for three seasons, what about my record…?"

"Forfeit three," interrupted Basil loudly.

"Ethel - Sunday's stock car race. Ethel is to drive her car painted as a big pink pansy."

"But I'm unethical Ethel. I'll be a laughing stock," said Ethel.

"Forfeit four: Nora," continued Basil. "No roller blading on Monday. Ethel

must walk to work in red high heeled shoes."

"High heels! I can't do them, I'll fall over. I'll be late for work. Oh no, not that!" said Nora.

"And finally," Basil announced, his face spreading into a wide grin.

"Forfeit five: All of Gran's Gang.

Tuesday, a notice on the church noticeboard with pictures. The notice is to read: "Gran's Gang are no more. They are going to act their age and be SENSIBLE'… and remember we will be watching you."

Basil stopped reading. He looked at Betty, they both smiled.

"You are enjoying this you old buffer,"

shouted Ethel. "You've done this on purpose. You've hidden your gnomes in the garage. This is blackmail. You just want to humiliate us, you've never liked us." Everyone started shouting at each other. It wasn't until Betty started crying that everyone fell silent.

"It's not us Ethel," sobbed Betty. "It's not. I just want things to be how they were."

"I know you do," said Mum quietly. "Come on everyone. You can do these things for Basil and Betty. You can take the medicine. I'll see if I can find a way of sweetening the pills."

Friday night

After Betty got so upset Mum persuaded everyone that they could do their forfeits to get Basil's gnomes back. Gran was not happy as they walked home. She called Betty a 'cry baby' and Basil a 'potato gnome'. Mum calmed her down by telling her that she and the gang would go to the club with her on Friday night for moral support and they'd keep a look out for who was there. She said if the gang spotted the same people at each event it must be the gnome stealers.

Friday night arrived and Gran went off early to get ready. She wanted to try a new Afro mix and she thought it would go down well with the clubbers. Mum and the rest of the gang arrived at about 11 o'clock. They didn't really have a good time. They all drank lemonade and kept looking at everyone in the club to see if they could see the gnome stealers.

Gran began her set at 11.30pm. She got the clubbers going. Her new Afro mix was a big hit. The dance floor was crowded. Just before midnight Gran faded down the Afro mix and slowly merged it into *"Please release me, let me go" by Engelbert Humperdinck.* The effect was startling, everyone on the dance floor stopped, they all stood still open mouthed looking at Gran. It was like time had stopped, someone started to boo. Mum knew she had to do something so she jumped onto the dance floor and danced crazily to *"Please release me."*

Mum shook her head, wiggled her hips and jumped around. She kept it up for the full three minutes of the song. The other clubbers were mesmerised, they didn't know what to do. They all just stood and watched. As the song finished Gran seized her chance, she faded the Afro mix back in and everyone started dancing again. Mum sloped off back to the rest of the gang. She heard Gran announce over the music "Freaky, freaky Friday folks. We can always make room for a freakie." Everyone cheered. Gran had got away with it. Mum drank a sidekick splash in one go.

Saturday

Winnie loves Saturdays; the day of her basketball games. She likes getting ready in the morning for the match in the afternoon. But not this Saturday. How could she miss two penalty shots on purpose?

"I can't do it. I won't do it," she said to Gran as they sat in the back of Ethel's car on the way to the game. "It's cheating. It's the thin end of the wedge."

Ada, Ethel and Nora decided not to say anything and they all drove on in silence.

When they arrived at the Sports Centre

lots of people were already there, including Mum.

"I've had a good look around already but I don't recognise anyone from the club last night. Do you?"

"We'll look around, you get ready" said Nora. "Good luck."

Mum, Gran, Nora and Ethel went to find their seats. They kept a close eye on the crowd.

The basketball match began. The Silvergrey Goddess Giants scored first, then Langrove Ladies equalised and for the first quarter the teams swapped baskets.

The second quarter began with a basket from Langrove Ladies and they went into the lead.

"I thought you said they weren't much good" said Ada.

"They're not usually," said Ethel. "I think they're having a lucky day."

Langrove's luck continued and at the end of the first half Langrove Ladies led the Silvergrey's by 46-38.

The second half started and immediately the Silvergreys were awarded two penalty shots.

"At last," said Mum, "now Winnie can do her forfeit."

Winnie stepped up and scored both baskets.

"What is she up to?" said Ethel. "I bet she's not going to do it."

Winnie did not look in the mood to miss anything. She bounced around the court scoring four baskets of her own and laying on another five for team mates.

"She is in good form today," said Nora. By the end of the third quarter the Silvergreys had a narrow lead of 62-60. The final quarter started with another penalty to the Silvergreys and Winnie scored both baskets again. On and on she went playing like someone possessed. Winnie scored another ten baskets on her own. The crowd were on their feet and cheering. Langrove Ladies were getting trounced. Still Winnie continued running everywhere

around the basketball court, even Mum
was impressed. She looked up at the
scoreboard.

Silvergrey Goddess Giants 104,
Langrove Ladies 76.

It was clear that the Silvergreys were
going to win. There was only one
minute left on the clock.

"One minute," said Ethel. "She's got so
carried away she's forgotten the
forfeit."

The clock ticked down, forty seconds,
thirty seconds, twenty seconds, ten,
nine, eight. Then the whistle blew for a
fowl against Langrove. Winnie grabbed
the ball. She took aim at the basket,
she missed. The referee threw her the

ball again, she took aim and missed again. The crowd groaned but Mum, Ethel and Nora cheered. Winnie had done her forfeit.

On the way home in the car Gran told Winnie how well she had played.

"Your best game of the season," said Ethel.

"But you left it a bit late for the forfeit," said Mum. "I thought you were never going to miss those penalties."

"I wasn't trying to," said Winnie. "I was just completely shattered."

Sunday

Everyone in our street knows when it's Race Day for Ethel. There is a lot of noise and activity from Ethel's house. This Sunday was different; Ethel had been busy in her garage - she had painted "Bingo Bruiser" as the forfeit said she should and she was not happy. All of the body of the car was pink and on the roof there were three green leaves with a big pink pansy in the middle. Ethel liked spray painting and she's a good artist. She'd quite enjoyed doing the car, she just didn't want to be seen driving it.

"Blooming Basil, blooming gnomes," she kept saying to herself, and then when she'd finished painting she looked at the car and smiled.

"Blooming car" said Ethel.

Anyway, Ethel's plan to do the forfeit was quite simple. She would do it but only once and quickly. She didn't want to be seen in a pink pansy car for longer than she had to.

"What about my image?" she kept saying to herself. "What about my fans, they'll think my attitude has gone."

So Ethel only entered one race this Sunday: the shortest race of the day, the 'Chaos Quartet.' Just four laps of the track with absolutely no rules about what you can and cannot do on the track. You can push other cars over, go backwards, even build special things onto your car to help you win. Ethel didn't usually enter this race because it can be a bit tough, but it's usually short so that was good enough this week.

When Ethel had finished painting her car she put a large blue plastic cover over it before she loaded it onto her trailer to take it racing.

"I have only got to be seen driving it. I'm not letting everyone else know I've gone soft," she said to herself.

Ethel arrived quite late at the stock car racing event. She still had "Bingo Bruiser" covered up. Mum and the rest of the gang were already there. They had been looking at the crowd. Gran spotted Harry Thistlethwaite and Winnie saw Wally Coulter. Mum wrote their names down. After a while it was Ethel's race.

"Race four shouted the announcer on the loudspeakers. "All cars to the starting line. Entrants for race four please get your cars ready. Race four, the Chaos Quartet, sponsored by Kirkland Estate Agents, Take the chaos

out of moving."

Slowly Ethel went round to the back of the Bingo Bruiser and pulled off the plastic cover. As soon as she did so she heard laughing and cheering from the other drivers.

"Are you sure you're at the right place," asked Bill Richards.

"Aren't you meant to be at the florists shop? "I hope it doesn't rain, we don't want to drown your pansy." said Peter Marr.

"Pretty, pinky pansy for pretty, pinky Ethel," sang Jack Watson. "Can I show the pretty little lady to the start line?" Everyone laughed again.

"I'll show you lot!" thought Ethel. Race four started and Ethel got away well in second place. After three laps she was still there, only Jack Watson in front of her. The biggest problem was dodging all the bits of metal that had fallen off the other cars in previous laps. Round the top bend Ethel knew she had to swerve past Peter Marr's car. He had come to a stop facing backwards after somebody had rammed him in the side. Ethel forgot she was driving a pink pansy. She was concentrating on winning. She would make Jack Watson eat his words. She revved the engine hard and pulled alongside him.

"Still with us flower girl," he shouted at Ethel as they both approached Peter Marr's stationary car. "Right," thought Ethel and she shouted at Jack: "Try this for Pansy Power," she said and she pulled a lever next to her steering wheel. Immediately the three green leaves on the roof of Ethel's car flew up into the air. They landed on Jack's car. He couldn't see where he was going and crashed into Pete's stationary car. Ethel sailed into the lead and cruised across the finishing line. "That's some powerful Pansy," shouted the announcer.

Ethel is still unethical.

Ethel was so pleased with her victory that she invited everyone back to her house to celebrate with a cup of tea. Mum said it would be a good opportunity for people to compare notes about who they had seen at the forfeit events. She said it might give them some idea about who was behind it all. As Ethel poured the tea Mum said she'd seen Donna and Young Gary at the nightclub.

"They go most weeks," said Gran, "and anyway, they're too nice to upset me."

"I saw Matt Rodgers," said Winnie.

"And I saw Sue and Ross Beesley," said Nora.

"What about the basketball?" asked Mum.

"Sue and Ross Beesley again," said Nora.

"Hmmm," said Mum.

"June and Bob Yates were there," said Ethel "but they go every week."

"And I saw that couple from round the corner in that corporate entertainment box."

The list moved onto who was at the stock car racing and Sue and Ross Beesley's names were there again.

"I don't believe this," said Mum. "It seems we have a couple of prime suspects: Sue and Ross Beesley. If we spot them tomorrow when Nora does her forfeit walk to work we may be closer to finding our blackmailers."

"Er,… well there's a bit of a problem there," said Nora. "You see I can't do the forfeit. It's not that I don't want to, it's just I can't. I haven't got any high heeled shoes. I don't wear many shoes, just roller blades and trainers. And the shoes that I do have are not red. I just can't wear red, it's not me and…"

"Don't worry Nora," said Mum. "I thought this might happen," and she produced a large carrier bag. "I've been around the charity shops and collected plenty of high heeled shoes. I've dyed them all red. You can take your pick Nora."

Nora looked shocked and disappointed. After a lot of grumbling she settled on a sling back high heel in shiny bright red leather.

Mum said she thought they looked "quite nice."

Monday

Nora was up earlier than usual. It would take her longer to walk to work. Luckily, the offices of Malcolm and Malcolm Insurance Agents (the offices she cleans) had moved to a brand new office block nearer to Nora's house. She reckoned she could walk there in about fifteen minutes, about the same time it took her to roller blade to the old offices.

Nora picked up her bright red high heels at her back door and forced them onto her feet.

"Good grief!" she said ."How do I walk in these?"

Mum had given her a "nice cotton bag" to carry her trainers in so that she could change when she got to work. Nora didn't really notice that the bag was red too. Mum thought Nora could "accessorise up a bit."

It was 5.45 am when Nora stepped out onto the street. She soon found how difficult it is to walk in high heels and she wobbled up the street past Basil and Betty's house. Her new shoes not only hurt but they made a noise as well.

"Oh no!" thought Nora. "It's bad enough wearing these things let alone waking people up in them." She tried to walk quietly but she was sure she saw upstairs curtains twitching as people looked out to see who was clomping down the street.

"At least I might see the blackmailers trying to keep an eye on me" she thought as she continued on her way. "Not many people are about at 6.00am so they might give themselves away." Nora carried on clomping down Norwood Avenue. She'd only seen the milkman and the postman. All she had to do was cut through All Saints' Walk by the church and she was nearly there, hardly anyone had seen her in her shiny shoes. Just as she turned the corner by the church she saw Mary Whitefleet hurrying along.

"Oh Nora" said Mary. "I didn't know you were coming."

"Coming where?" said Nora.

"On the church outing to Blackpool," Mary replied.

"I'm not," said Nora.

"Oh, it's just that you're all dressed up, and out for our early start. I thought you were coming with us. Nice shoes."

"I'm not coming," Nora said again. "And no these shoes aren't nice."

"Oh, no need to be like that!" said Mary Whitefleet. "I just thought you looked particularly lady-like this morning, what with your shoes and matching bag and things."

Nora looked hard at the bag for the

first time. She did not answer Mary but moved on past the church gate as fast as she could. It was then she noticed the coach for the church outing. People were sitting ready to go and other people were arriving for the day trip to Blackpool. At least twenty other people had seen her in her noisy, shiny, red shoes. She was sure she heard Bob Yates whistle at her from the bus. Nora tried to retain her dignity as she hurried on but she lost her balance on one heel and stumbled off the pavement.

"Oh la la la!" she heard shouting from the bus. Nora would have given up there and then, but she knew she had

nearly completed the forfeit. She
struggled on for the next fifty yards
round the corner by Kirkland Estate
Agents and across the road into the
offices of Malcolm and Malcolm
Insurance Agents. Nora threw her high
heels into her cleaning bucket.

The Mystery is Solved

Nora finished cleaning the offices of Malcolm and Malcolm as usual by nine o'clock in the morning. Ethel had agreed to give her a lift home in her car so that they could all be back at the Wainwrights' house in time for the "planning meeting" called by Mum. "Right, we've, - you've done four out of the five forfeits and you've all done very well. Just the notice to prepare for the church notice board and we can get Basil's gnomes back," said Mum. "I know you really, really don't want to put that notice up so let's see what clues we've got so far. We've got less than 48 hours to find out who's behind all of this. We still have until midnight on Tuesday."

"Looking at the names we've collected we only have two people as suspects: Sue and Ross Bessley. They've been seen at the club, basketball and the racing. Did you see them watching you on your walk to work this morning Nora?" asked Mum.

"No I only saw the milkman, the postman and that silly Mary Whitefleet whittering on about clothes. I bet it's her. She's always been jealous of your gnomes Basil. I bet she's got your gnomes. Let's get the police onto her. That would show her."

"Hang on Nora we can't do that," said Ethel. "Even if we don't like her we've got no evidence."

"And anyway," said Gran, "she wouldn't have taken Basil's gnomes. She might be a bit snooty but she has got some taste."

Everyone started to laugh except Basil and Betty. Mum bit her finger gently.

"Moving on," Mum said. "It seems we have no real suspects. We'd better start planning the notice for the church notice board."

"Wait a minute!" shouted Nora suddenly. "Sue and Ross Beesley, yes I did see them this morning. They were on the coach I think. After bumping into Mary Whitefleet I had to walk past the bus going on the church outing. I bet they were on it. It was very full. I didn't stop to look but they don't usually miss church functions.

"They're on the church committee," said Gran.

"And they do that stall at the church fete," said Winnie.

"And Ross Beesley said how much he liked my Phil the Irish Fluter," said Basil.

"And Sue Beesley's just been elected to the Parish Council," said Betty.

"That's why they wouldn't steal anything," said Mum. "I'm not sure about this. Sue and Ross are good people. What have they got against Basil and Betty or the Gang? They came to your barbecue the other night."

"No they didn't," said Betty. "We asked them but they didn't turn up, they never said a thing.

"They're jealous they missed such a good do," said Gran.

"Let's call the police," said Winnie.

"I'll get my car, we'll go round their house," said Ethel.

"Hang on, hang on. I'm not sure about this," said Mum. "We can't go round to see them if they are on the coach half way to Blackpool. Let me deal with this. I'll pop round this evening when they get back. I'll even peek in their garden to see if they've got any gnomes. We can all meet back here tomorrow morning at the same time. And just in case we need it I'll type out a notice for the church notice board."

Tuesday

"Where is she?" asked Ethel. "It's gone ten o'clock and we've got to get on with things." The Wainwrights, Mum and the rest of the gang were waiting for Nora to get back from work. They had to talk about doing the final forfeit and putting the notice on the church notice board. Nora was late and nobody was happy. Mum had already explained that she had gone to see Sue and Ross Beesley. She found out that they weren't on the bus to Blackpool and Nora hadn't seen them yesterday morning because Sue had been in bed with the flu. Ross had stayed at home to look after her. He had had the flu the week before and that is why they'd missed Basil and Betty's barbecue. Mum even went into their garden, not a gnome in sight. They had not stolen Basil's gnomes and they were not blackmailers.

"I'm glad it wasn't them," said Mum, "even if you do have to do the final forfeit."

Nobody replied but the silence in the room was broken by Nora as she rushed in, still wearing her roller blades.

"I've got it, I've got it. I know who the blackmailers are. I've solved the mystery!" shouted Nora. "Look at this."

Nora pulled a handful of scrap paper from a plastic bag she was carrying.

"I found this, early this morning in one of the offices of Malcolm and Malcolm. It was in the bin next to the photocopier."

Nora showed everyone some sheets of paper with holes cut out in them. They were sales notices about houses that are being sold; the sort you get from estate agents when you're moving house.

"Look at this, look at this," said Nora. "This one has had the word 'granny' cut out from the description about granny flats. And this one has the words 'further instructions' cut out."

"This one is missing lots of single letters," shouted Winnie.

"And 'pink', 'painted' and 'stock' are all missing from this one" said Gran.

"Quick," said Mum, "get the notes Basil and let's see if it's the same paper."

Basil produced the blackmail notes and everyone could see that the letters and words had come from the scraps of paper that Nora had found.

"So we know who did it," said Nora. "Because if you look at the letter head on this stuff you'll see they've all come from Kirkland Estate Agents and we all know who works there."

"Julia Stansfield!" shouted everyone.

"Yes. And these other papers come from the office of the chief accountant of Malcolm and Malcolm, Morgan Stansfield - that husband of hers. The Stansfields are the blackmailers."

"I knew it, I knew it," said Basil. "You should have heard what he said to me that night he came round to complain about the barbecue."

"And she was so rude," said Betty. "I've never liked her."

"But wait, it gets better," said Nora. "When I found these I couldn't believe it and I got a bit delayed with my cleaning, so I hadn't finished before people started arriving for work in the office. I was just finishing off and putting these papers in my bag when I heard Morgan Stansfield on his telephone. He was laughing away and being very jolly. I didn't catch everything he said but I did hear him say, "today's the deadline - got them at last - good for the parish, tell the newspapers and thanks for your help Councillor Bolam."

"So he is in on it as well," said Mum. "Well I never!"

"Well done," Nora said Betty.

"Brilliant," said Winnie.

"Congratulations," said Gran.

Everyone agreed Nora had been very clever and observant.

"Now you won't need to post that silly

notice," said Ethel.

"You will if you don't get my gnomes
back," shouted Basil. "We still haven't
got them back."

"But we can go to the police now,"

said Mum.

"They won't be interested," said Basil. "And do you really want to remind them about what happened at the barbecue." They have suspicions about your sound deck Ada and they know about your car Ethel. No, you'll have to post that notice."

"I don't know, maybe not," said Mum. She had been looking at the scraps of paper carefully. She had matched up most of the words and letters missing with the forfeit notes and she had discovered there were a lot more extra words missing.

"Look," said Mum. "It looks like

they've cut out the words for the final ransom note. There are some words here that they will have to put on the next note to tell you where your gnomes are. Look they've cut out 'house' 'sale' 'find' 'garden', '64 Kimble Road'.

"That's the big detached house that's up for sale," said Mum. "Donna was interested in it. It's got a big garden but Donna said it was too pricey."

"That's where your gnomes are Basil," said Gran. "They've hidden them in the garden of an empty house. Brilliant."

"And I know how we can get them back," said Mum.

Mum told everyone about her plan and
they all knew what they had to do.
Then Mum rushed home to find Donna
from next door. She told Donna that
she had to telephone Julia Stansfield at
Kirkwell Estate Agents. Donna told
Julia that she wanted another look at
64 Kimble Road, that she was still
interested in buying it. Julia could not
resist the possibility of a sale and she
agreed to meet Donna at 64 Kimble
Road at 2pm. Donna told Julia that
Mum would be there as well to help
her make up her mind.
While this was being arranged, Nora
roller bladed back to the offices of

Malcolm and Malcolm. She told the
security man she had left her cleaning
stuff out and she had to put it away.
On the way out she told a secretary
that she had just found a note on the
stairs for Morgan Stansfield and that it
must have been dropped by someone.
The note said: *"Meet me at number 64
Kimble road in the garden at 2.15pm."*
The secretary said she'd make sure
Morgan got it.

Gran, Ethel and Winnie each did their
bit. They all separately telephoned
Councillor Bolam to tell him that they
thought they had seen squatters in
number 64 Kimble Road. Gran told him

it would reduce property values and Ethel mentioned next month's Parish Council elections. Councillor Bolam agreed to meet her at number 64 at 2.15pm. The trap was set.

At 2 o'clock Mum and Donna met Julia Stansfield at 64 Kimble Road. Julia took them on a tour of the house. She showed them the fitted kitchen and the en-suite bathroom. She kept going on and on about 're-sale value' and 'upcoming area'. At ten minutes past 2 Donna said the main attraction of the house was the large garden. Julia agreed.

"It's so nice to have so much space,"

she said.

"And it's been so well looked after," said Donna. "I think I can see some garden gnomes."

"So can I," said Mum. "There's one playing a golden flute and, Oh look, there's a gnome with a fishing rod."

Julia looked nervous. "Oh yes," she said. "I spotted those as I came in. Very nice if you like that sort of thing but I'm afraid they are not being sold with the house. The owners are taking those with them."

"Oh that's a shame," said Donna. "But can we go into the garden and have a look?"

Julia opened the back door and she led Donna and Mum onto the rear lawn. At the same time, from the side of the house, Morgan Stansfield and Councillor Bolam arrived.

"Morgan, Councillor, what are you doing here?" asked Julia, looking shocked and surprised.

"We know," came a loud shout from the shrubbery around the lawn, and Gran, the gang and Basil and Betty Wainwright jumped out of their hiding places. They surrounded Julia, Morgan and Councillor Bolam. They harangued them about what had happened. Nora showed them the scraps of paper. Basil

and Betty picked up their gnomes.
There was a lot of shouting and
arguing. After about ten minutes Mum
and Councillor Bolam came to what
they described as a "workable
compromise."

It was agreed that the police would not
be told about the blackmail notes and
that Gran's gang would not appear on
any notice boards or be mentioned at
any future Parish Council meetings.
Julia and Morgan apologised to Basil
and Betty about their gnomes. They
said they were never going to keep
them and they offered to buy Basil a
new gnome for his collection. Julia said

this was a 'well negotiated settlement.' Donna told me later that she'd never seen my Mum so angry. "I don't know," she said. "It's never dull living in this street with your Gran and her gang."

Wednesday

A new notice arrived on the church notice board on Wednesday morning, it read:

*Basil and Betty Wainwright would
like to thank all of their friends
who helped in the recovery of their
lost garden gnomes.
Particular thanks to
Ada, Winnie, Nora and
Ethel- Gran's Gang.*

Gran's Gang have solved a mystery.

Adrian Townsend

Lives in Oxford. He likes playing golf,

football and dominoes as well as

writing stories.

He can be contacted on E mail at

Hidip@aol.com

If you enjoyed this book Look out for

other stories by the same author

including

Naughty Lessons
Gran's Gang
Gran's Gang Go To Spain

and

Teachers' Tales